# Disney
# PIRATES of the CARIBBEAN
# JACK SPARROW

## The Siren Song

by Rob Kidd
Illustrated by Jean-Paul Orpinas

Based on the earlier life of the character, Jack Sparrow,
created for the theatrical motion picture,
"Pirates of the Caribbean: The Curse of the Black Pearl"
Screen Story by Ted Elliott & Terry Rossio and Stuart Beattie and Jay Wolpert,
Screenplay by Ted Elliott & Terry Rossio,
and characters created for the theatrical motion pictures
"Pirates of the Caribbean: Dead Man's Chest" and
"Pirates of the Caribbean: At World's End"
written by Ted Elliott & Terry Rossio

## DISNEP PRESS

New York

Printed in the United States of America

First Edition
7 9 10 8

Library of Congress Catalog Card Number: 2005905547
ISBN 1-4231-0019-0
www.DisneyPirates.com

# The Siren Song

Captain's Log:

Our proud ship _Barnacle_ set sail from Tortuga a few weeks ago. I must admit ~~we~~ Arabella and Fitzwilliam are quite the landlubbers, but things are improving. We took on two crew members, a Creole chap called Jean and a Mayan named Tumen, when we washed up on what we thought was a deserted island, after a vicious storm—a raging beast of one—started by the dreaded Captain Torrents, incidentally. Alas, we also picked up Jean's raging beast of a cat, a creature he claims is actually his sister under a mystic's curse. I fought off and, of course, soon defeated the rampaging Captain Torrents practically single-handedly, and found a whole lot of treasure. I cleverly deduced that the magnificent sword is now in the hands of the fearsome pirate Left-Foot Louis, and we are making fair speed after him.

# CHAPTER ONE

"As we all know," Jack Sparrow began, facing his crew, who stood before him on the deck of the *Barnacle*, "the diabolical pirate captain we are following lost his right foot in battle."

Jack tossed a perfectly polished onyx stone around in his hands. It was the stone used as a glass eye by the legendary pirate, Stone-Eyed Sam, and Jack had retrieved it from the lair in Sam's ruined pirate kingdom. Jack kept it with him at all times as a memento of his most recent adventure. He thought it might make a nice piece of jewelry: maybe a necklace or something. He stuck the stone in his pocket as a swelling wave heeled the deck. Jack grabbed a line for balance, ducked as the mainsail jerked toward him, then continued his story, hardly missing a beat.

"The captain, the notorious Left-Foot Louis, swiftly slew his fearsome boatswain, quickly lopped off his foot, and had it expertly reapplied to his own leg by the ship's cook, the equally notorious pirate Silver, who, having recently sailed the high seas with a certain doctor, had henceforth become skilled in the art of limb-replacement surgery. Only after said surgery was it evident that Louis, in his panic to get his appendage back, severed the wrong foot."

Fitzwilliam P. Dalton the third, Jack's

aristocratic crewmate, laughed obnoxiously.

"Oh, rubbish." Arabella, the crew's first mate and a former barmaid on Tortuga, laughed.

Another wave rocked the boat. Arabella clung to the railing to maintain her balance. Fitzwilliam landed on his rump, while Tumen and Jean, the young sailors Jack had met on Captain Stone-Eyed Sam's island, scurried to steady the ship. Jack, the only crew member who had somehow remained steady despite the swaying of the boat, scowled.

"Your attention!" he barked. "Your captain is speaking."

"Jack, my friend," Fitzwilliam said, picking himself up off the floor, "you may *think* you are a captain, but look closely around you. This is surely *not* a ship, and we are *hardly* a crew."

Jack stepped up to Fitzwilliam. He was a

whole head shorter than the aristocrat, but commanded as much, if not more, respect.

"Question my authority again, mate, and you'll be having this discussion with Davy Jones," Jack said. "On this ship, you call me *Captain* Jack Sparrow."

"Fine . . . Jack," Fitzwilliam said with an uncharacteristic smirk.

Jack huffed and moved toward the bow where Arabella stood staring out over the bowsprit. Despite her tousled hair and bedraggled clothing, Arabella looked very much like the lady she was. She had a delicate face toughened by all the things she'd seen and done.

"Missing Tortuga much, Bell?" Jack said sarcastically.

"Yeah, sure," she responded with equal sarcasm. "I miss me dad terribly." She ran her hand along the boat's railing and stared dreamily out to sea.

Jack hoisted himself up onto the bow and swung his legs around so that they dangled on either side of the bowsprit—the long pole that extended out over the water. It was a glorious day at sea. The warm sun shone brightly, making the crystal clear water sparkle. Jack took in a deep breath, and the salt air filled him with a happy feeling of adventure. This was much better than traveling as a stowaway, as he had before. And far nicer to be at sea than scrambling for a crust in the rough-and-tumble town of Tortuga.

Jack surveyed the *Barnacle*. Arabella had settled onto the deck, sitting cross-legged with her back against the foremast. Her tangled auburn hair fell in front of her face as she studied Tumen's astrolabe, a navigational device that used the stars as a way to determine a ship's position. She seemed deeply engrossed, and for Jack that was a good thing: the more crew members who knew how to navigate, the better. Fitzwilliam, calmer now, secured the lines and watched the horizon while Jean and Tumen went about their duties. And best of all— Constance, the foul-tempered cat that Jean claimed was really his sister under a mystic's curse, was nowhere to be seen.

*Yes*, Jack thought proudly, *this is a right trim ship*. No matter that it was full of splinters, the sails were tattered, and a few spots in the galley below and over the berths leaked when it rained.

Jack jumped back down onto the deck and clapped his hands. "Back to my story," he said.

The crew moaned, but Jack rolled his eyes and continued despite the protest.

"Upon discovering the error Silver had made, Louis quickly had the cook-cum-surgeon-cum-pirate tossed overboard. But Silver was under the protection of Sirens, who attacked Louis and used their power to fuse his botched job into place forever. He was clawed across the face by a Siren's talons, which is why he now has three scars running from his right eye over his nose to his left jawbone.

"Oh, ye will believe anything," Arabella said dismissively.

Jack swiveled all the way around to face her. "Then, pray tell, why do *you* think the man in question has two left feet?"

Arabella did not take her attention away from the astrolabe. "Accident of birth," she said flatly.

"We are obsessing over the wrong details," Fitzwilliam put in. "Louis is a dangerous pirate, and we should be concerned with how we will defeat him and secure the Sword. It will not, rest assured, be easy."

"You're not frightened, are you, boyo?" Jack asked with a smirk. "I warned you this was no mission for the lily-livered and pampered."

"I should think I have already proven I am neither," Fitzwilliam snapped, turning his head sharply to glare at Jack.

"No need to get huffy," Jack said. "Any *sane* man would be afraid of going up against Louis. So perhaps you're saying you're crazy. Hmm. That's a bit worrisome."

Fitzwilliam sighed and shook his head. He wasn't going to take Jack's bait this time.

Despite his arguing, Jack knew Fitzwilliam was right. Louis would not give up the Sword. Not when it was rumored to grant great power to whomsoever wields it—and omnipotence when it is united with its sheath. Of course, Jack badly wanted the freedom that having the Sword would provide. But equally important, he needed to keep the sword out of the hands of dangerous pirates, like Louis and Torrents—and especially out of the hands of the evil Davy Jones, who was said to rule the seas.

A gust of wind billowed the mainsail, and the heavy boom swung around. Jack quickly jumped out of the way, toppling into Fitzwilliam. They both went sprawling on the deck, and a wave washed over the railing, soaking them. Jack smoothed his long dark hair and scrambled to his feet.

"Big wave," Jack said.

Fitzwilliam got up from the now-slippery deck more slowly and carefully. "Why is the water getting so rough? It was not calm earlier, but it was also certainly not this violent. And there is nary a cloud in the sky, so it cannot be that Torrents has escaped and is stirring up the sea with his storms."*

"Perhaps not Torrents, but it could be Louis," Jean said. "Who knows what power the Sword wields, even without the scabbard? And in the hands of Louis, a little bit of power will go a long way."

Jean continued. "He is certainly a vicious man, diabolical and fierce. The only thing about your story that was not accurate, Captain Jack, is how the pirate became marked with those facial scars."

"Oh?" Jack scoffed. "And how are *you* such an expert?"

"We met him," Tumen said, returning to his place at the wheel.

*Jack and the crew defeated the notorious Captain Torrents, whose anger stirs storms, in Vol. I: *The Coming Storm*

Everyone turned toward the helm to stare at Tumen. Then a yowling sound filled the stunned silence. Constance leapt down from her hiding place behind the mainmast and landed right in front of Jack, finally showing her mangy self. She let out an angry but frightened hiss.

# CHAPTER TWO

Jack's eyes narrowed as he stared at Constance. The shabby cat's tail flicked slowly, purposefully, as she stared back. For a moment there was a standoff. Then Constance let out another hiss; her back arched and she bared her teeth. Jean bent down and picked her up. "Ah, *ma petite*," he crooned to the flustered cat, petting her matted coat. "My sister is clearly nervous enough simply *hearing* Louis's name. *Please* don't make things worse for her, Jack. She's suffered enough."

Jack smirked, then took off his bandana and brought it to his chest. "Please accept my most heartfelt apologies, m'lady," he said to the cat, with an exaggerated bow.

"Oh, enough already," Arabella said to Jack (and for that matter, to Constance, too). Arabella gazed up at Tumen, who rested a hand lightly on the wheel. "What do ye mean, you *met* Left-Foot Louis?" Arabella asked.

"Just as I said," Tumen replied. He relaxed against the helm, as the sails billowed and the ship made a steady course in the sea, which had calmed down considerably.

"Not only did we meet him," Jean said, "we faced him in battle. We barely escaped with our lives."

Tumen nodded. "He is a fierce fighter."

Jean petted Constance a moment, then

he glanced at Tumen as if he wanted his permission to tell the story. Tumen shrugged.

"It was not quite a year ago," Jean said, leaning against the rail and holding Constance tightly in his arms. "We made port in Martinique, and we were unloading the cargo. Precious stuff, those spices. Worth their weight in gold—literally. And quite handy to have on hand in the kitchen." He scratched Constance under the chin. "You do love your cumin and coriander in your Creole rice, don't you, *ma soeur*?"

"Get on with it," Jack barked impatiently.

"We were working with the longshore-men at the docks," Jean explained. He put Constance back down on the deck and she immediately licked her paws and began washing her face. "They seemed a rough and rugged band, but they often are, so I thought no more about it."

"That work does tend to attract a hardened lot," Fitzwilliam commented, nodding.

"How would you know?" Jack asked. "One whiff of the wharf and you'd probably faint."

"*Would you let Jean speak?*" Arabella complained. "Go on, Jean."

"Thank you, *mam'selle*. We unloaded crate after crate," Jean continued. "The sweat beading on our brows, trickling down our backs. We were nearing the end of the load, and I was making my way down the gangplank balancing a trunk on my back. Constance, eager to see the town, I'm sure—she's always so curious about far-flung places—dashed between my feet."

"Jean fell," Tumen said.

"*Vrai*," Jean said with an embarrassed shrug. "I rolled all the way down the gangplank. And then—this part is bad—the trunk crashed open when it hit the dock. Luckily, this trunk held none of the rare and precious spices we were carrying—it was part of the silk shipment. So I was relieved."

"Relieved to have dropped *silk*?" Fitzwilliam asked.

"Silk doesn't break," Tumen explained.

"Still, anything ruined would come out of my miserly pay," Jean said. "I wanted to gather up the fabric before it could get dirty or torn."

"I had already begun to collect the silk," Tumen said.

"But then all worries about my money flew out of my mind when I realized I'd fallen at the feet of the *foreman*. *Mon Dieu!* I would catch it for sure, now. The foreman would complain to the owners, who would complain to my captain. . . ." Jean shook his head at the memory.

"They don't like their cargo spoiled," Tumen agreed.

"Understandably so," Fitzwilliam said.

Jack opened his mouth to make a wise-crack comment to Fitz, but noticed a warning look from Arabella and kept quiet.

"Seeing as I had fallen next to the foreman's left boot, I thought the best course of action would be to move to the right . . . away from the towering brute! So I did—and slammed into *another* left foot! I had heard all the legends about the dreaded pirate with the two left feet," Jean said. "I had no doubt as to his identity."

"Did he know that you knew?" Arabella asked.

"And more important, did you know he knew that you knew?" Jack added. "You know?"

Tumen looked at Jack, confused.

"Louis stared down at me," Jean continued. "I gazed up at him, too afraid to move.
In a low, gravelly voice, he muttered not to
move a muscle or make a sound. I thought I
was done for."

"I didn't know then what was happening,"
Tumen said.

"I cannot see that mad pirate allowing
anyone to live who could identify him,"
Fitzwilliam said. "However did you escape?"

Jean scooped up Constance and cradled
her to his chest. "With the help of my dear
sister. Constance leaped into the air and tore
her claws clear across Louis's face. That gave
me the chance to roll out from under his
feet. It was she who saved me."

"And well she should," Fitzwilliam said.
"She was probably attempting to make up
for the fact that it was her fault you were in
such a predicament in the first place."

"I didn't blame her," Jean protested. "And she scratched him so badly, he still bears those scars today. So, perhaps Sirens were involved in the fusing of his flesh, but *non*, it was *my sister* who marked him."

"What happened next?" Arabella asked, completely absorbed in the story.

"I shoved him backward," Jean said, "hard as I could. His wig had slipped off when Constance had lunged for him, and there it was—his famous bright red hair—for all to see."

"I let out a cry of warning," Tumen said. "Our crew swarmed to the railing."

"That was when everyone aboard our ship realized Left-Foot Louis had done away with the *real* foreman and the *real* crew. It was his *own* shipmates unloading—and *stealing*—our cargo."

"Clever chap," Jack said with a smile.

"Our brave and loyal shipmates piled out of every nook and cranny of the ship and threw themselves into the melee," Jean said. "It was awful. Knives flashing, fists flying.

"Then, Left-Foot Louis ripped open his shirt to display his thick chest covered with strange tattoos that looked like quill markings. He pointed to me and to Tumen—"

"We were fighting side by side," Tumen said.

"—and he shouted that he's finished a thousand men and has a marking on his chest for each one. He swore we would regret that day. He was going to find us, slaughter us, and he would skin my dear Constance alive."

Constance's fur puffed out, and she hissed again.

"Oh, don't be afraid, dear one," Jean crooned. "We won't let any such thing happen." He looked back up at the others. "Louis managed to take out two members of our faithful crew and escape. We have lived in fear of him ever since."

Jack whistled through his teeth. "Well, that there is *some* story. How much of it is *true*?"

"All of it!" Jean said.

"He's not lying," Tumen added.

"To my point earlier," Fitzwilliam said, "this only bolsters Louis's reputation as driven, cruel, and quite mad."

"We can't let him get the Sword," Arabella vowed. "It's too dangerous."

"Isn't that *exactly* what I said before?" Jack said. "Keep up, lass."

He looked at her more closely. She was a greenish shade of pale and looked faint. "Are you sure you're all right?" he asked.

"I'm fine," Arabella said. She stood and

leaned against the railing, waving him off and facing the water. "It's just a bit of seasickness."

Before they could press Arabella any further, a faint, ghostly sound wafted out of the water. It held the crew—with the exception of Jack—frozen for a moment. Then, as suddenly as it arrived, the sound floated out over the sea once more. The crew stirred, as if they were emerging from a dream, the *Barnacle* began to rock violently, and when the crew looked up, they saw before them a tall mountain of an island.

"Um, where did that come from?" Jack asked.

"I can assure you," Tumen said, looking up from his navigational tools, "that island was not there a moment ago."

# CHAPTER THREE

$\mathcal{T}$umen stepped away from the wheel to make way for Jack. Fitzwilliam was looking through his spyglass toward the island.

"It is difficult to make out," Fitzwilliam said. "Almost as if the island is there, but at the same time . . . not. It looks like nothing more than a cloudy mist through my glass."

Draping his arm across the top of the wheel, Jack gazed ahead. The sun was making a slow descent, and the horizon was striped in shades of gold, pink, and purple. "Sail toward it," he commanded.

"Are you mad?" Fitzwilliam asked.

"No. But I am a bit tired of being asked if I am," Jack replied.

"Why would we sail toward it? We have no idea where it came from, nor what exactly it is," Fitzwilliam persisted.

"Well, Fitzy, when anything happens at sea that is out of the ordinary like, oh, say a huge island appearing out of nowhere, it would probably be wise to ascertain that it happened for a reason, and that reason can often, though not always, lead anyone willing to explore it to great power and treasure. Besides, I am captain here. Savvy?"

"Aye, aye, 'Captain,'" Fitzwilliam snapped obnoxiously.

"I don't know about this," Tumen said.

Jack just set his jaw, pointed toward the island, and the crew sailed on.

"I guess we know where the rough seas

were coming from earlier," Jean said. "Islands dropping into oceans will probably do that to calm waters."

Just then the wailing sound started up again. It was strange and mystifying, but it was also beautiful. At least most of the crew thought so.

"What is that god-awful noise?" Jack said.

"I think it's pretty," Arabella said, "and so . . . sad," she continued, clearly on the verge of tears. The rest of the crew looked completely mesmerized. Jack looked puzzled.

As the sound died down, the crew shook off the sleepy feeling the song had inflicted upon them. But before the effects had completely worn off, the *Barnacle* began to rock more violently than it had before. And from the turbid waters around them, like a cannonball fired from below the sea, shot an enormous roaring beast.

"Kraken!" Arabella shouted, as the eel-like body of the beast slapped down on the ocean around them, attempting to crush the *Barnacle*.

"No! The Kraken is much larger, has tentacles, and smells like death. . . . This is something different!" Tumen said.

"But it looks . . . and smells . . . no less dangerous," Jack shouted. "Grab your swords!"

As the crew quickly prepared for action, the monster lurched and slapped itself down on the water, showing its face. Its huge jaws looked as if they could easily take a bite out of the *Barnacle*, and they were lined with rows of teeth that were set layer-upon-layer, like a shark's. Its ruby-red eyes glared angrily at the crew, and as it hissed it sprayed them with a green slime that smelled like long-dead fish.

"Oh!" Arabella shouted.

The monster dove in toward the *Barnacle*, and Jack nodded to Fitzwilliam. Just as the monster was mere feet away from the boat, Jack jabbed his sword directly into one of its eyes and Fitzwilliam hit the beast in the side. A pink fluid sprayed from the eye wound and oozed out. The creature roared and recoiled for a moment. Laying limply on the water in what looked like a pink oil slick, it seemed as though the beast might be down. But then it squirmed its huge body, which was at least the size of the *Barnacle*, and straightened itself high in the air, turning toward the *Barnacle* and lunging again for the boat.

Jack yelped and jumped back, then with hardly a thought, he jumped up onto the ship's railing and steadied himself in a ready position.

"Jack! What on Earth are ye doing?" Arabella called out to him.

The creature was clearly in attack mode and Jack was right in its path.

"Going to the belly of the beast," Jack said with a wink, sword in hand. As the monster lurched forward, Jack jumped off the side of the boat and onto the creature, grabbing its fins for stability. The crew gasped as the monster whipped its body around in an attempt to free itself from Jack's grip. But Jack was holding on tightly.

The creature opened its huge mouth and angled its head in an attempt to swallow Jack whole. But like an animal trying to lick its own neck, the creature was unable to reach Jack, who was just beneath its jaws.

"Get the boat away from this here beastie!" Jack shouted to his crew.

"What?" Arabella shouted. She couldn't

hear well over the roar of the creature and the rush of the water. The wound in the creature's eye continued to leak fluid, and fishy green slime dripped from its jaws, fully covering Jack and causing him to lose his grip.

"Boat. Out. Now." Jack repeated what he had said before.

"We cannot hear you!" Fitzwilliam said.

Jack's right hand continued to slip off the monster's fin, and in a desperate attempt to get a better grip, he let go, then quickly grabbed the fin again, tearing it clean off the body of the beast. The creature roared louder than it had up till now, and the crew gaped in terror.

"I think we'd better get the boat out of here," Jean yelled to Jack.

"Good thinking!" Jack shouted back, now hanging from just one of the creature's fins.

"What?" Arabella asked, not able to hear Jack over the chaos.

"Just get going! Go!" Jack shouted. Then the beast reared up and slammed Jack down on the surface of the water. Jack was able to hold on, and when the creature broke the surface again and straightened its body as it had before, yowling like mad, Jack took his sword, inserted it just below the monster's jaw, and slid down the length of the creature, cutting the beast in the process. The thick skin of the creature split open to reveal bluish guts covered in dark blood. It tossed its head like mad, spraying its green slime all over the surface of the water, then collapsed on top of Jack.

The water was still for a few moments as the crew watched, stunned, and waited for Jack to surface. But there was no sign of him.

"Oh, my . . ." Arabaella said, putting her hand to her mouth.

Then, suddenly, from behind the ship, a loud splash sounded. Something had shot out of the water again.

"Jack!" Fitzwilliam shouted, genuinely pleased to see him.

"Who were you expecting? Davy Jones?" Jack quipped.

The crew looked out onto the water where the carcass of the mighty beast lay in an oily pool of monster juice.

"Well," Jack said, "looking on the bright side, we now have boatloads of meat for the rest of the journey."

# CHAPTER FOUR

The crew sailed away from the butchered sea beast, which sank slowly to the ocean depths. They were entering the thick of the fog that surrounded the island which had appeared on the horizon, but the island itself was miles away yet. The ocean was still and silent again, the only sounds heard were the creaking boards and the slap of the waves against the *Barnacle*'s hull.

And then, that *other* sound again . . . the beautiful, haunting, lovely, maddening sound.

Jack wondered if it could be the howling of sea beasts, like the one he had just slain.

"Come near my ship, beastie," Jack yelled out toward the ocean, waving his fist as a warning, "and I'll do to you what I've already done to your mate."

He stood at the ready, but as he scanned his crew, he noticed that they were not responding at all. While he was prepared for another battle, they were slack and relaxed.

Arabella stood at the rail, staring gloomily out to sea. Fitzwilliam sat on a barrel, pulled his sword from his scabbard and used his neckerchief to slowly polish it, making long, smooth strokes. Tumen picked up the astrolabe Arabella had laid on the deck and seemed to be studying the stars, which was odd, since none had appeared in the sky yet.

Jean petted Constance over and over, the cat lying limply in his arms.

"What *is* all this?" Jack scolded. "We have a ship to—"

His voice broke off, as the sound, floating along the wind, became louder. It was like a song, but not exactly. There were no words, just sounds. It was hard to tell if it was one voice or many. And though it was clearly being sung, the melody wasn't very song-like—no repeated phrases, no hummable tune. Jack wasn't sure if he was hearing it with his ears or if somehow the sound had burrowed into his brain and he was hearing it from inside his head. It was wrapping itself around him like the tentacles of some sea beast.

Jack threw his head back and forth violently, trying to shake the sound out. Then he stood up straight, enduring the sound, and cleared his throat. "Mates," he said to his crew, "it's high time for—" He suddenly ducked as the boom swung toward him.

"Hey!" Jack cried, yanking on the line. "Tumen, Jean. Look alive there, mates."

The two able-bodied seamen ignored him, so he left the helm to lash the rope to the cleat at the stern, making a tangled mess of the excess. "I'll fix that later," Jack muttered.

*Thwack!* Jack jumped at the sound of all three sails suddenly furling.

"What the—" he sputtered, wondering how he would set them right all at once. He strode to the center deck. "Jean, Tumen," he barked, "trim the jib and the foresail. Arabella, Fitz, you tackle the main."

No one moved.

*Whomp!* Jack jumped again and stared up incredulously as the sails unfurled, returning to their proper positions.

Something had clearly taken control of the ship—something powerful and *invisible*. Could it have something to do with the strange song? Jack wondered. "Well, at least the sails seem to have sorted themselves out. More than can be said for you lot!" Jack said, glaring at his crew. He opened his mouth to deliver a severe tongue-lashing, but then noticed the wheel at the helm twirling madly. He dashed back to it and tried to get it under control. "A little help would be nice," he called.

No response.

He turned his back on the deck in order to face the wheel directly, struggling with it. It suddenly seemed to have a mind of its own. Every time he yanked it one way, it yanked itself back the other. He had the oddest feeling that someone was under the ship pulling on the rudder, forcing the wheel to guide the ship away from the island on the horizon.

Jack closed his eyes tightly in frustration. He released the wheel to pull his bandana from his head and wipe his face. He watched dumbfounded as the wheel spun around and around like a wayward top. It then stopped dead still. Just as he reached for it again, it whirled frantically, first one way, then the other. He yanked his hand back from the mad dance of the wheel.

"Fine, be that way," Jack shouted at the wheel.

None of his crew members had budged a single inch. Jack would have thought they'd been mystically turned into statues if they weren't each absently, languorously, and silently continuing their activities. The setting sun cast long shadows across the deck.

Jack jumped down in front of Fitzwilliam.

"To arms!" he shouted, expecting Fitzwilliam to raise his sword and rush to the bow. But the young aristocrat just continued running his neckerchief up and down the blade. Jack huffed in frustration. He was getting nowhere.

Jack crossed to where Arabella stood gazing out to sea. "What is so bloody fascinating out there?" he asked her.

She didn't answer, didn't move, just gripped the rail, her long hair lifting in the wind.

"Well, if you want to go all statuey, lass, that's your prerogative. But I have a ship to sail here," Jack said, stepping away from her.

He turned and joined Tumen at center deck. The young sailor was making adjustments to the astrolabe. "I hate to break this to you, my good fellow," Jack began, "but I can't see what use this device can be if you hold it upside down."

Tumen behaved as if he hadn't heard a word.

Jean was petting Constance—or more correctly, attempting to. The cat had slithered out of Jean's hands and onto the deck. She lay sprawled in a way that made her look like a limp rag doll. It was unusual behavior for the feisty, albeit nasty, feline. Yet Jean's hands continued to move as if he were still holding her, rising and falling, rising and falling.

"What is wrong with you lot? Have you forgotten that we were just minutes ago nearly killed by a sea beast? Step up, now. These are dangerous waters!" Jack barked.

Jack took a step toward them, but suddenly the song that had been blaring seemed to shift pitch and become much softer. Then Arabella shivered, Jean clasped his hands together, Tumen stopped manipulating the astrolabe, and Fitzwilliam's polishing slowed to a halt.

The melody was still dancing about the boat, but now it was only a whisper. Jack felt as though the song were an entity that had just wound its way across the deck and was now heading back out over the water.

The crew appeared to be getting back to its normal self, and then, suddenly, the sound increased markedly. The crew went stiff again, and the sails flew up and down the masts. The boom swung back and forth, and the lines untied themselves. Jack went into frantic action, dashing all over the ship, reaching, pulling, yanking, shoving—and above all, shouting. He was on his own for now. Despite his commands, not a single crew member responded.

Panting, sweating, and furious beyond belief, Jack Sparrow leaned heavily on the wheel. It had set its own course, away from the island, and he'd given up trying to change it. At this point, *any* destination was better than jerking about this way and that.

"Might as well see where we're headed," he murmured. He pulled out his pocket compass and peered down at the instrument, but it was getting dark. He needed to light the lanterns. That was usually Arabella's job, but it wasn't likely she'd be taking that on this night.

The compass needle flickered back and forth without rhyme or reason. It wasn't pointing north. Nor was it pointing south or east or west. It was just spinning aimlessly.

"Hmm. That's probably not good," Jack said, matter-of-factly.

He shoved the compass back into his pocket. "Well, let's try this." He glanced at the standing compass. That needle also made a slow circuit around and around and around, like a sped-up clock. The instruments were as useless as Jack's so-called crew. He crossed to the rail to better see his mates. They all seemed to have fallen asleep. Jack wasn't sure if it was any worse than having them awake and useless.

Grumbling, Jack strode to the bow, taking care not to *accidentally* kick anyone (though he did so a few times). As he peered into the oddly starless night, the wind picked up, pushing the *Barnacle* speedily along.

# CHAPTER FIVE

*C*ome morning, a bleary-eyed Jack stood wearily at the helm, glaring at the rising sun. He had not gotten one wink of sleep. Between the strange melody that had come and gone all night long, and the phantom island, which was now once more nowhere to be found, sleep did not seem an option. Especially when he was clearly the only one in a suitable position to captain the *Barnacle*.

"How can you sleep through that incessant drone?" Jack complained to his snoring crew, though the sound seemed so faint now that he could hardly hear it.

"Look alive, mates!" He strode across the deck, clapping his hands loudly as he paced among the crew. He stopped at the bow, turned and stared down at the crewmates, shaking his head. Not one had so much as rolled over.

He bent down over Fitzwilliam. "Ahoy, there!" he shouted into the sleeping boy's ear.

"What? Who goes there?" Fitzwilliam sat bolt upright, clutching his now extremely polished sword.

"And a good morning to you, too," Jack said. "Has Prince Charming gotten enough beauty rest? Good, because now it's time to get back to work!"

"Work?" Fitzwilliam asked, confused.

"The running of the ship, you spoiled,

soft-handed cretin!"

"Do not insult the honor of a Dalton," Fitzwilliam warned. "You will regret it."

"Okay. One, I do not have time for this, and two, well, there doesn't need to be a two, does there?" Jack said flatly. "Now, wake up the rest of this group of useless cargo so we can get this ship back on course toward that disappearing-appearing-reappearing island. That's an order," he shouted. Then he added, snootily, to Fitzwilliam, "And even the aristocratic Daltons know that disobeying a captain's order will result in a court-martial."

"Here we are again with this captain business," Fitzwilliam groused. "You're no captain, Jack."

Jack raised an eyebrow. "Would you care to repeat that?" he said, a warning tone in his voice.

"We are five young people and a cat . . . type . . . thing . . . lost at sea," Fitzwilliam replied.

Jack scowled, but as he opened his mouth to reply, he heard a scream from the other end of the deck. It was Arabella, and she'd been woken up suddenly by Constance, who was standing up on her hind legs, hissing at the Tortugan barmaid.

"Constance!" Jean cried out, also waking suddenly. "You're scaring the *mademoiselle!*" The cat shuffled away on her hind legs, and Jack and the rest of the crew stared in wonder.

"Does she do that often?" Jack asked Jean.

"*Non, monsieur,* she's never done it before."

"Well, it's pretty bloody odd if ye ask me," Arabella snapped, dusting off her weathered dress.

Tumen was now at the wheel to guide the

rudder, and Arabella moved beside him—and away from Constance—to continue her navigation lessons. Jean moved to the mainsail and Fitzwilliam to the bow.

Then, the song returned. It seemed to Jack to have a physical weight to it. More like a presence than a sound.

Jack pulled his compass from his pocket. It had been working fairly well a moment before, but now it was broken: no revolution around the face, no pointing in multiple directions—it was doing nothing at all. He held it starboard, he held it port, he held it toward the bow and then toward the stern. It never moved.

"Blast it!" Jack said, sliding his compass back into his pocket and resisting the urge to hurl the disobedient instrument into the sea.

He went to the helm. "What course are we making?" he asked Arabella.

Arabella just shrugged.

Jack saw that the needle on the ship's compass slowly swung back and forth.

"Tumen, my friend," Jack said, smiling and draping an arm around the young sailor. "You're a regular Galileo with navigational tools, land-sea-position things and what have you. Can we get some help here?"

"There're no stars now," Tumen said. "I need the night sky."

"I wish you'd mentioned that last night," Jack said. "Now, why didn't I ask you *then*? Oh, right," he added sarcastically. "You were too busy sleeping as if you were in a coma."

Jack strode away from the helm and began pacing the deck. "So," he began, "we don't know where we're going, but we seem to be headed there at quite a clip. We have sea beasts prowling these waters and a discordant sound that gives one the sensation of fingernails running over slate. If that weren't enough, a phantom island drops in now and then. This is brilliant." He threw his hands in the air.

"All right, my mates," Jack announced, continuing to pace the deck. "I'm willing to put behind me your most unseemly, unworthy, slackish, brackish behavior of the night previous. But let us get something straight. If you're going to sail on the *Barnacle*, you're going to pull your own weight. Or we'll leave you at the next port," Jack looked around at the expansive ocean around him, then finished, "wherever that might be. Savvy?"

The singing sound grew much louder.

"I am beginning to question why we are even here," Fitzwilliam stated.

"Pardon me, Fitzy," Jack said, "but was it

not you who demanded passage aboard this ship? Was it not *you* who vied for your right to sail with *us*?"*

Fitzwilliam rolled his eyes.

"I guess the intermittent spells of waves we've been encountering have rocked the little sense you may have had right out of that priceless head of yours, eh, lad?"

"I warned you once, I shall not warn you again," Fitzwilliam said. "Do not insult my honor or that of my family."

"A bit touchy this morning, aren't we?" Jack said. "You ask me, *I'm* the one who should be suffering from a foul disposition. I've had no sleep, and my charges sat staring into space as the ship went mad around me."

"A ship can't go mad," Jean scoffed from the rail.

"I beg to differ," Jack said, spinning

* Yep, Jack is right. See for yourself in Vol. 1: *The Coming Storm*

around to address Jean. "And if you had managed to stay awake last night, you'd know precisely what this ship had gotten up to. Now, can't we *please* just get back to planning the mission?" Jack said, clasping his hands together and bowing forward.

"Mission?" Fitzwilliam repeated disdainfully. "This is a fool's errand at best."

"How's that?" Jack turned on his heel to face Fitzwilliam. "As this is *my* mission, I believe you are calling *me* a fool."

Fitzwilliam shrugged. "So be it."

Jack took a step toward the tall boy. "Might I remind you yet again, *aristo-brat*." He enunciated every word precisely and rolled his *r*'s for good measure. "You begged to come aboard. Insisted upon it. And you were as eager to reunite the Sword with its sheath as any one of us."

"That was before I realized what madness

such a mission is," Fitzwilliam said.

"A few days ago you discovered what it felt like to conquer a violent, bloody, not to mention cursed, pirate. You felt the freedom of discovering treasure and sailing the seas free from the constraints of family Dalton. Then just yesterday you watched yours truly," Jack said, pausing to wink at Arabella, "slaughter a raging sea beast. You've done things that wizards and kings through the ages have only dreamed of doing," Jack said with a convincing amount of passion. "This is the mission of a lifetime and you know it," he finished.

"Not my lifetime," Fitzwilliam answered.

"Let me remind you who is captain here," Jack said.

"And who decided that? Not we. Is a captain not elected by his crew?" Fitzwilliam crossed his arms and took a wider stance, planting his feet firmly on the deck.

Jack stared at the belligerent boy. The others stayed quiet, although it was unclear if their silence was because they were afraid to interfere in a fight between Jack and Fitzwilliam, or if the astonishing indifference brought on by the song was continuing.

"If you will recall," Jack said smoothly, "I appointed myself captain, seconded by all of you. And besides," he added with a grin, "*I'm* the one with the compass."

"A compass that does not work. Not unlike your mind. This is not a ship. It is a decrepit boat. You are not a captain. You are a lunatic," Fitzwilliam said.

"Oh, that was very unwise, Fitzy," Jack snapped, his hand instinctively gripping the sword he wore at his side.

"Oh, put your sword away. You are so dramatic," Fitzwilliam said dismissively. "I tell you this mission is doomed, and I refuse to link my name to such folly. We do not have the resources to take on a pirate such as Louis."

"Of course we do!" Jack protested. "And you thought so, too, up until oh, let's see, *moments ago*. We are *not* abandoning this mission."

"If I cannot change your mind, then do take your own advice and set me ashore at the nearest port," Fitzwilliam said.

"Oh, and why would you want to do that?" Jack asked.

"I plan to take my portion of the treasure we have already found," Fitzwilliam said. "I will buy myself a position as an officer in the army. I will ensure my valiant leadership and bring the Dalton name to glory."

"Hah!" Jack shook his head, laughing. "*You?* First of all, friend, let's face it—

you're not exactly, how shall I put it? 'Leader' material. Not to mention that you're here with us because you were running from that very life," Jack said. "Now, who's the lunatic?" he whispered to Arabella.

"How dare you impugn my honor!" Fitzwilliam unsheathed his sword in a swift move.

"'Impugning'? There's no 'impugning' going on here. What are you talking about?" Jack said.

"You will guide this boat to a port," Fitzwilliam said, his voice growing hard, "where I shall disembark."

"Look, Fitzy, it's not like I'm desperate to keep you," Jack said mildly, waving his sword around carelessly. "You're not much of a sailor. But out of very *principle*, I do not take orders from my crew. Besides, I am not taking a detour from Louis's trail to drop you off."

"You will do as I say."

"No. I. Won't," Jack said.

"I repeat, sir, you will do as I wish, or pay the price!"

"You forget yourself, 'sir,'" Jack said mockingly. "Let me remind you again. Despite your protests, I am, in fact, captain here. And onboard ship, the captain's decisions are law."

Fitzwilliam charged forward and lunged at Jack. Jack nimbly leapt up onto the gunwale and grabbed the ratlines leading to the crow's nest. Missing his target, Fitzwilliam stumbled. Jack gripped the ropes and swung around the ratlines, landing a hard kick on the tall boy's backside. He toppled into the mainmast, hitting his head hard against the wood and crumpled to the deck.

"Oh, my," Arabella exclaimed. But she

didn't move from the helm.

"Sorry about that, Fitzy," Jack said, leaping down from the ratlines to land beside the unconscious boy. "But you gave me no choice."

Jack propped Fitzwilliam up against the mainmast and lashed him to it, taking care that all his knots were secure and proper.

"Now, you'll go nowhere," he said as he wiped his hands together, an indication of a job finished and well done.

Constance crept back on the deck and delicately sniffed Fitzwilliam.

"Glad that's taken care of," said Jack, clapping his hands together briskly. "Maybe he'll talk more sense when he comes to. You know how these aristos are—all vapors and fits of madness."

"I agree," Tumen said.

"Why, thank you, my friend," Jack said,

smiling.

"No, I agree with Fitz," Tumen replied, never taking his eyes from the astrolabe, which he held up as if he were reading a night sky—despite the bright sun blazing down on them.

"Me, too," Jean said.

Constance yowled, presumably in agreement.

# CHAPTER SIX

As Jack's crew decided to give up the pirate chase, the song continued.

"Blast it all! Stop this ear-bending *noise!*" Jack shouted. He clapped his ears, shook his head, and went back to pacing the deck, taking care to step over Fitzwilliam's outstretched legs.

"Who are you yelling at?" Jean asked.

"Them. The singing ones! The song people! Oh, never mind," Jack said, giving up.

"I hear nothing, *monsieur*, but your ranting," Jean said.

"I also hear nothing," Tumen said.

Jack turned to Arabella. "What about you? What do you hear?"

"Wind. Waves," Arabella replied. "It's beautiful." She looked moved to tears.

"Well, folks, then clean out your blasted ears," Jack cried.

"I think the insanity of this mission is getting to you," Jean said.

Jack gaped at Jean.

"I agree," Tumen said.

Jack pointed at the boys. His mouth opened and shut a few times as if he were going to say something but was too appalled to find the words. Finally he said, "Well, of all this crew, it figures the young ones would lose courage and loyalty soonest!"

"Well, not exactly 'soonest,'" Tumen

pointed out, "Fitz lost it first."

"Point taken," Jack agreed.

"There are more important things in this world than this dumb Sword," Jean said.

"Jean is correct," Tumen said.

"I'll tell you the merit in all this," Jack said, leaning against the mainmast to steady himself, yet still swaying with the rolling deck. "One!" He held up a finger. "The sword we are looking for grants great power. Two." He held up another finger. "With that power, we could rule towns, cities, populations, counties, countries. Three." Another finger in the air. "That sort of power inevitably yields great wealth—the greatest of which is freedom, the ability to have to answer to *no one*." Jack stressed, "Well, no one, except for me—and I will go easy on you, I promise." He held up all five fingers.

"Oh, and did I mention the power part? Besides," he added, adjusting his head scarf. "The Sword is probably very becoming and will look lovely hanging in the captain's cabin. I can't think of a worthier cause."

"A *much* worthier cause," Jean grumbled, "would be to restore my sister to her human form."

"Oh, that drivel again. Will you cut that out?" Jack said. He watched Constance wriggle out of Jean's overzealous embrace. She skidded a bit when she landed but quickly regained her footing. She scampered across the deck to the plate of fish heads Jean had put out for her and sniffed them.

"Right now," Jack said, "that nasty cat is the only crew member behaving at all normally."

"There is *nothing* normal about my sister being a cat!" Jean exclaimed. "And now, *monsieur* Sparrow, we will turn this ship around and head for the bayou shack of Tia Dalma. She put this curse on my sister, she can have it removed."

"Sorry, lad, I'm not into the whole mystic idea. This Tia Dora . . ."

"Tia Dalma."

"Yes, 'Tia Dalma' does not sound like someone I'd want to cross, being that she creates beasts as wreched as this cat-thing here."

Constance's ears flattened. She yowled and spit at Jack.

"Back atcha, luv," Jack said.

"Do not speak to my sister in such a tone," Jean said. "And now, we set sail for Tia Dalma."

"But first, we must set a different course," Tumen interrupted. "I need to be left on the sandy white beaches of the Yucatan. I need to return home."

Jack threw up his hands in exasperation. "Another county heard from!"

"No," Jean said, striding toward the helm. "We must go to Tia Dalma." He shoved Tumen aside, grabbed the wheel, and yanked it to the right. The boom swung quickly around, careening into Jack and dragging him with it.

"Um, hello?" Jack shouted from the boom. As Tumen and Jean fought over control of the boat, the boom shifted back and forth.

"Yucatan."

"Tia Dalma."

"Um, Captain. Onboard. Commanding you to stop!" Jack barked, as he was dragged back and forth across the deck. Then he finally let go of the boom, rolled to the rail, and stood, careful to stay out of the way of the swinging boom. He strode over to the fighting kid sailors, intending to take control of the wheel.

Jean and Tumen stopped fighting each other and turned to Jack. "Don't come any closer," Jean warned. "You're not getting ahold of this wheel." A strange glint came into his eyes.

"You're looking a little crazy there, Jean," Jack said. "You know, wild-eyed, foamy at the mouth, and all that."

While Jean was distracted by Jack, Tumen grabbed the wheel.

"Tumen, off that wheel!" Jack ordered.

Wanting to be in control of the wheel himself, Jean turned to tackle Tumen. Jack smiled and knocked Jean on the back of the head with his elbow. Tumen turned to see what had struck Jean, and as he did so, Jack smiled and ducked. The boom was swinging in from behind him, and it landed square in Tumen's jaw. Both young sailors were out cold.

Jack dragged Tumen and Jean to the mast, mumbling to himself, and lashed them beside the still-unconscious Fitzwilliam.

Jack stood back up and stretched. Although the sun was still beating down on them, the strange fog that had earlier surrounded the disappearing island rolled in again. It wrapped itself around the ship. As Jack peered through it, he noticed large green fins breaking the surface for a moment and then disappearing quickly below.

For a moment he thought they might belong to other sea beasts. But the fins he had just seen dip beneath the waves were far too small for that. As the fog cleared, the island, which they must have traveled miles and miles from by now, mystically reappeared.

"Wonderful," Jack said, heading for the helm. "Sea creatures, reappearing islands. What next?"

# CHAPTER SEVEN

"Do not fear!" Fitzwilliam shouted. He strained against the ropes that kept him tied securely to the mast. "I shall lead you into glory! Fall in behind me, men, for Fitzwilliam P. Dalton the Third and his men will be victorious!"

"Now who's delusional?" Jack muttered to himself. "'This is not a ship.' 'You are not a captain.'" Jack mimicked Fitzwilliam's taunts. "Well, lad, seems *you*, not *me*, are the bloody lunatic!"

Jack scanned the ocean, looking for a sign of the mysterious fins he saw dip beneath the waves, or anything else unusual. The misty island was on the horizon again, and the last time it had appeared, the *Barnacle* was attacked by a sea creature. Jack turned toward Arabella, who was leaning on the railing. This had become something of a habit for her, Jack noticed.

"You still with us, lass?" Jack asked, noticing the glazed-over expression on her face.

Arabella said nothing. She just continued to stare out at the sea.

Jack sighed.

Tumen stomped his feet as best he could from his position at the post. He was screaming and yelling in his native tongue, but occasionally Jack understood words like "home" and "now."

The song was getting loud again, and as it

wound its way through the boat Jack could almost *feel* it. As it passed them, Tumen and Jean grew limp, and their bodies seemed to sway to the song.

"Home," Tumen moaned. "Let me go home."

"Oh, Constance. We've got to lift your curse," Jean cried. "Tia Dalma . . ."

Constance let out a howl, stood up on her two hind legs and, bizarrely, "walked" below to the galley.

"That again?" Jack asked, puzzled by the cat's behavior. There was something strangely comic about it, but also something deeply disturbing.

*Thwack!* The flying jib at the bow of the ship backwinded. The imbalance of the sails made the boat tip dangerously to starboard. Jack skidded across the deck and caught himself just before he tumbled over the rail.

He gripped the ratlines and straightened up.

"Oooh, you'd like that, wouldn't you?" he said to the *Barnacle*, convinced now that the ship itself was out to sabotage his mission. "Well, it will never happen." He grinned while his restrained crew continued to chant, moan, and shout, and Arabella continued to clutch the port rail, her sad eyes never leaving the horizon.

"It's the sea, doll. Just the sea," Jack said, frustrated by her sudden obsession with the ocean. "Seen one, seen them all. Waves, horizons, open air. Not much else to look at besides that foggy island that might or might not be there depending on when you look, and the occasional odd tail of a sea creature that may or may not be a beastie ready to attack us."

Jack took a step toward her, hoping, though he knew it might be in vain, to get her attention. But the ship was still back-winded, and he slipped backward. "I'll be back in a moment, doll. Must attend to the jib," he said.

Keeping a hand on the rail, he hurried to the bow. He ignored the crew, neatly leaping over them. Then he sat astride the bowsprit, muttering to himself while he inched along the pole to release the wayward sail.

Salty spray stung his eyes, and he almost slipped twice due to the slickness of the wet bowsprit, but he finally made it back to the deck.

"Are you going to say anything today, Bell?" Jack asked.

Silence.

He waved his hands frantically in front of her face. "Hello there!" he yelled, exasperated. Gesturing to the subdued crew, he said, "Even if this lot here does not want to complete this mission, it's still you and I, lass. You and I who decided to do this. You and I who found the scabbard. You and I who secured the *Barnacle* and set sail and defeated Torrents.* It's you and I who are going to find this blasted sword, and keep it out of the hands of thieves, pirates, and most of all, Davy Jones. And it's you and I who will be free to do whatever we wish with its power!"

"It doesn't matter . . ." Arabella's voice trailed off. "None of it matters."

Before Jack could respond he was distracted by Constance, back on deck from the galley. He shook his head in disbelief.

"What do you mean, 'none of it matters'?" he asked. "*All* of it matters. Every last blasted moment of it. We're partners, me and you. You said so yourself the night we met."

* All in Vol. 1: *The Coming Storm*

Constance looked over her shoulder at Jack and Arabella and let out a snarky meow. Jack's eyes widened as he watched the cat walk two-legged over to the cup of tea Arabella had left beside the stovepipe the day before—before everything went crazy on the ship. Constance leaned forward—still balancing on her hind legs—and tried to lift the cup with her paws. Over and over she made the attempt, letting out annoyed mews at her inability to grasp the handle of the cup.

"Of all the odd things I've seen in my day, this is up there," Jack muttered. He walked over to Constance, who was now trying to steer the ship's wheel. He scooped her up and tied her to the mast as well, right beside Jean. The cat's mewing joined the rest of the crew in forming a painful off-key symphony of groans.

All the while, the melody coming off the sea rose and fell. The rhythm of the song seemed to match the swell of the waves, the pitch of the ship.

Jack peered up at the sails, then out to sea. Through the haze of gray fog rolling off the island, he again spotted several green fins. As they dropped just below the surface, he gripped his sword, preparing for the worst— another attack by a vicious beast. But he also thought the fins could just as easily belong to some kind of large fish.

The fog began to wrap around the ship, and Jack noticed that they were closer than ever to the dark island that kept appearing. Jack stomped to the helm. Then he whirled to glare at the three boys and the cat tied to the mast. He cocked his head as he watched their antics. Clearly it was the song that had driven them mad. But why wasn't *he* affected? And why not Arabella? Or *was* it affecting her?

He turned to face the barmaid, who was still staring out to sea. "I don't know what your problem is, Lady Misery," he said, "but at least you're not trying to change the course of the mission."

"Jack, I—I want my mother."

Jack stared at her, surprised. "The lady speaks!" He furrowed his brow. "But she speaks nonsense."

"I do, Jack. I want to be with my mother." Arabella finally pulled her gaze from the sea and faced him, her eyes wild.

"Your mother, eh?" Jack raised an eyebrow. "Well, best schedule a visit to the graveyard, dear. Everyone in Tortuga knows your mum is dead."

"If death is the only way for us to be reunited, then so be it."

Jack watched, stunned, as Arabella gripped the railing, hoisted herself up, and turned to him. Then, without another word, Arabella threw herself overboard.

# CHAPTER EIGHT

"*O*h, brilliant," Jack cried, as he watched Arabella fall into the sea.

He stared down at the water. Arabella disappeared below the surface but then quickly bobbed back up, gasping. Her hair streamed out behind her, and her long skirts floated up around her head. But as the heavy fabric of her dress soaked up the seawater it weighed her down, and she began to sink again.

*Only one thing to do,* Jack thought, tossing his vest onto a cleat for safekeeping. He threw the boat into the wind to stop it, leapt up onto the railing and dove into the churning blue sea.

He plunged in with a splash and quickly broke the surface, scanning for Arabella. He shook his head to get the shaggy wet hair out of his eyes and spotted the top of her head just above the water.

He swam to her, hoping she wouldn't resist his effort to save her. Coming up behind her, he grabbed her head and tilted it up out of the water so she could breathe. With his other hand he gripped her firmly around her shoulders, positioning her so that she lay nearly on top of him. Then he kicked hard, floating on his back, and pulled her along with him toward the ship. She seemed unconscious, but her eyes were open and blinking. She wasn't actually fighting him, but she was much heavier than he had expected—it almost felt as if she were being pulled in the opposite direction. Could her dress have snagged on something underwater?

Jack suddenly screamed out. A sharp stab had made him jerk his hand up and out of the water, releasing Arabella. He treaded water and checked his hand. Blood streamed down into the warm Caribbean Sea. Jack's eyes bulged. Teeth marks. Like human teeth, but much sharper.

Arabella was out cold and sinking again. Jack watched hopelessly as her head slipped below the surface.

He muttered something, took a deep breath, and plunged down. Once below the waves, he opened his eyes and tried to focus. Underwater, everything was a blur, but he could still see Arabella slowly drifting toward the ocean floor. He kicked hard and was quickly by her side. He wrapped one arm around her and used the other to paddle, bringing them back up toward the surface. He had to hurry.

Then he realized that something was, in fact, dragging her down.

Colorful fish swam in front of him, seaweed smacked him in the face, and his own kicking churned the water—all these things obscured his ability to see what was pulling Arabella deeper and deeper. And he knew he couldn't hold his breath very much longer.

He kicked hard, trying to yank Arabella out of the grasp of the unseen obstacle. He wrapped both arms around her to make sure he didn't lose her again. He reached as far as he could to strengthen his grip around her and found himself suddenly staring into a surprising—and surprisingly beautiful—face. Long, flowing hair the colors of the sea drifted around the strange girl. Her pearly skin made him think of the inside of an oyster shell, and her eyes glowed like moonlight. She was perhaps the most gorgeous girl Jack had ever seen. And he had seen countless pretty girls in his day.

Gorgeous.

Until she opened her mouth wide—and released a bubbly hiss.

Jack reared back in shock, and in this moment of confusion loosened his hold on Arabella. The fish-girl grabbed Arabella's shoulder and tried to yank her out of Jack's arms.

Jack didn't need another clue to know that this underwater stranger had bad intentions. Those sharp teeth of hers definitely matched the bite on his hand, and now that he was less startled he noticed that she was in fact a girl, but only from the waist up—she had a shimmering, scaly tail the rest of the way down her body. A mermaid!

They had to get out of there—fast! Back up to the surface for air and back to the ship for safety! There were stories about mermaids. Many of these tales told of mermaids that were very sweet and innocent. But there were other tales of sinister mermaids who had aligned themselves with Sirens. Jack quickly deduced that this one was part of the latter group.

Clutching Arabella tightly to his chest, Jack quickly curled his body into a ball and then sharply flung out his legs, kicking the mermaid square in the chin. She reeled backward, and Jack swam as fast as he could for the surface with Arabella heavy and lifeless in his arms. He glanced down to see if the mermaid was gaining on him, and his heart thudded hard.

The mermaid who had attacked Arabella

was there, but she wasn't alone. Scores of other mermaids were gathering below—and they were all headed straight toward Jack!

His lungs were already nearly bursting, but he forced himself to push hard for the surface. He knew he couldn't fight off all those creatures, and he wouldn't be getting any help from Arabella.

He swam rapidly, lungs burning, muscles straining, Arabella's weight slowing him down. He fought against his tiring arms and his exhausted legs, determined to get both himself and Arabella out of that water. He burst up into the air, gasping and sputtering. But it wasn't over yet—he still had to make it to the ship.

The water rippled around him, and he knew it was from the legion of mermaids making their way toward the surface, their green fins flapping as they sped up to him. He couldn't slow down now. He kicked and kicked, dragging Arabella along, creating a wake.

Finally, he reached the ship, and never softening his grip on Arabella, hoisted himself onto the ladder that hung over the side. Steadying himself, hooking his feet into the rungs, he managed to shift Arabella so she was over one shoulder. He grabbed the rail of the ladder and scurried aboard.

Jack heaved himself and Arabella onto the *Barnacle*. He laid his shipmate down, and then, panting, he collapsed. His chest rose and fell as he regained his breath. As soon as his lungs were full, he knelt beside Arabella, who was pale, bloated, soaking wet, and what concerned Jack most of all—not moving or breathing. He opened her mouth and placed his lips firmly on hers, exhaling into her, willing her to breathe, determined to awaken her.

*After all that*, he thought, *she can't have drowned. Not after all that!*

Arabella coughed and sputtered, and Jack yanked her upright, pounding on her back so she'd cough up all the seawater she'd breathed in.

The moment she got her bearings, she stood and raced back to the rail.

"Oh, no, you don't!" Jack shouted, chasing after her. He grabbed her around the waist just as she was about to jump overboard— again. "I risked my life getting you back onboard. I'm not doing it twice."

"I must get to my mother!" Arabella wailed. "Release me at once!"

"I didn't see your mum down there with the Scaly Tails," Jack said, dragging her over to the mainmast. "You'd be wasting your time.

And I'd have to get myself all wet again rescuing you." He lashed her to the mast with the others.

"The reason men made ships," he complained, "was so that they didn't have to get themselves drenched going from place to place." He took the ends of his shirt and wrung the water out of them. He stood in a soggy puddle. "If I've ruined these boots," he warned Arabella, "someone—and I think we both know who I mean—*someone* is going to make me a new pair."

Jack stalked back to the helm, leaving a trail of wet footprints and seaweed in his wake.

# CHAPTER NINE

*J*ack smacked the wheel. He walked to the mast, circling around his newly deranged crew members. "So," he began, pacing back and forth in front of them, "it has recently become clear to me that the Sirens, or something like them, are the reason for all of this bizarre, strange, and utterly unacceptable behavior. This of course indemnifies you all on some level—though not entirely—but it does not solve my more immediate problem, which is how do I overcome this trial and get you all back to normal." He glared at Constance, who was sitting with her paws crossed angrily, "Or, as normal as possible.

"It also does not explain why I seem to be the only one remotely aware of this Siren song, nor does it explain why I have not been affected by it." Jack stopped and thought for a moment.

"It *does* explain the sea beast."

He paused again and concentrated.

"It does *not* explain the appearing-disappearing island.

"It does explain the presence of the song, whether you can hear it or not."

Jack rubbed his chin thoughtfully.

"So! You see, we have more items unanswered than answered."

The bound crew members were limp and stared slack-jawed and expressionless at Jack.

"And it's clear none of you are hearing any

of this, so I am basically speaking to a mast," Jack said.

"Anyway," he continued, "about these Sirens . . . I don't know why I didn't realize it before. We've all heard the stories, the legends. Every sailor lives in fear of being called to their watery grave by the Siren's song. He leaned over the side of the ship and cupped his hands together. "I guess I just thought they'd be a bit more on *key*," he mused.

Just then, the song wrapped itself around the ship once more. The crew perked up.

"For the glory of the Crown and the Dalton name!" Fitzwilliam shouted. "I must report for my commission at once! Why are you detaining me?"

"Well, you see, Fitzy," Jack said, kneeling down beside the delirious boy. "There *is* no commission. There *is* no Crown. And after today I am not even sure there is a family Dalton. Everything you've been saying is out-and-out rubbish." Jack was enjoying turning the tables on Fitzwilliam, who consistently insisted that Jack was not a captain.

Jack stood up, then stumbled a moment, dizzy and light-headed. He steadied himself by grabbing the mast over Fitzwilliam's head. "Must have not quite recovered from my dip in the ocean," he muttered.

"Mother!" Arabella pleaded. "I must see my mother! I must!"

"Bell," Jack said quietly, "I really don't think it's a good idea for that request to be granted."

"Tia Dalma!" Jean moaned. "We have to go see her!"

"I believe your friend Tumen will argue that," Jack pointed out. Tumen nodded angrily in agreement. "And I'd hate to cause a rift between such good mates. So I shall refuse you both, in the interest of your friendship. We're keeping to our original course."

Constance had stopped yowling and hissing. She simply sat there, staring at the ropes wrapped around her and gazing up at Jack defiantly. From the twitching of her tail, he was pretty certain he'd pay for her confinement later.

"And you," he began to address the cat, who bared her teeth, "oh, never mind."

Jack started suddenly and flapped his hands quickly about his ears, as if he were trying to shoo away the song. He lowered his wet bandana over his ears and tightened it, hoping it would help muffle the sound.

It didn't.

Jack groaned in frustration and gritted his teeth. The ship was drawing ever closer to the island, and Jack was beginning to think that if this was where the Sirens or mermaids, or whatever they were, *wanted* him to go, then he should make every effort to *avoid* heading toward it.

He gave the wheel a try—hoping it would work this time—and was thankfully surprised that the rudder responded to his touch. "Okay now, Scaly Tails," he shouted out to the sea, "thank you for your hospitality. So glad you'd like us all to stick around your strange disappearing island, but sorry, it's getting late, must be going. Savvy?"

Peering at the instruments, he realized that although the compass seemed to be working, he had no idea which way to guide the *Barnacle*. The boat had been pulled in so many directions between here and there—between the first encounter with the sea beast and now—that he had no idea where he was. Further, with his crew tied to the mast, he'd have no help adjusting the sails to catch the winds. He thought that once the starry night appeared, Tumen would be able to help him with navigating. . . . Then he looked over at Tumen, who was drooling all over himself and stuttering, "Home! Home!"

"No help there," Jack said. "Well, actually, thinking about it more carefully, this can't *really* be all *that* hard. All I truly want to do is get out of here. It doesn't matter where I wind up, as long as it's far from sea beasts and the Scaly Tails."

As Jack tried to figure out how to maneuver the boat away from the island, the song grew even louder, filling Jack's head completely. It was nearly impossible for him to think of a plan, a direction to take. Any thought he had was crowded out by the wailing of the song and the shouting of his crew.

"All right, that's it!" Jack stalked away from the wheel. "I've had it with all of you!" Jack shouted. Turning to his crew, he continued through gritted teeth, "And I do mean *all* of you."

There was only one thing to do. He had to face the creatures who were tormenting him and entrancing his crew. One way or another, he had to stop the singing. That was the only way he'd be able to break the hold over his ship and his mates. If the Scaly Tails were too cowardly to come to him, then he'd be more than willing to join them on their turf.

He strode to the prow of the ship and planted one foot on the bowsprit. "All right, Scaly Tails," he bellowed out to sea, "I know who you are. I know the game you're playing. I'm ready to fight for my crew! So, come out . . . and play with old Captain Jack Sparrow!"

Sudden silence.

Then, Jack heard the lapping of gentle waves against the hull of his ship. Finally, a delicate, pale hand broke the water. A finger was lifted and it beckoned Jack into the sea.

# CHAPTER TEN

Without hesitation, Jack dove into the water. A powerful current swept over him, and he felt himself being sucked downward. He opened his eyes wide, but the water was spraying his face, stinging him so badly that he needed to squint. He felt the rush of water all around him, and it became clear that he was inside a whirlpool or something very much like one. He was spun around and dragged deep into the ocean, deeper than he'd ever been before. He could feel himself

descending, and the little bit of light he could see through his now barely opened eyes was waning. Down he went, his hair whipping around, the underwater world swirling into a frenzied blur.

Just when he thought his lungs would burst, Jack was spat out into a vast cavern at the sea bottom. "Ouch!" he shouted as he landed. He lay gasping on shell-covered sand.

"Hey," he murmured, "there's air down here. And light." Given these strange facts, Jack was not sure if he'd actually landed at the bottom of the sea, or if he'd been transported to another dimension entirely.

Slowly, he pushed himself up and gazed around.

The huge cavern walls shimmered with the refraction from the turquoise water, each tiny ripple sending glints of light across the ceiling. Little pools full of translucent shells and exotic fish dotted the sandy shore. Black coral formed bridges and thrones throughout the dark, damp, cavernous space that dripped and oozed with slime.

Three mermaids with bright blue tails lay in the center of the cavern atop a slick boulder. They stared at Jack, their dark eyes haunting and intense. Around them, in shallow water, were hundreds of mermaids with green tails. They also stared at him intently. Relegated to a far corner of the cove were a dozen or so red-tailed mermaids. Jack couldn't tell where they were looking, but he thought it safe to assume that they, too, were staring at him.

Jack stared back. He'd never before seen such a sight. "All these beautiful mermaids." He smiled. "Creatures of legend and lore, right in front of me! What an exciting adventure, indeed!" he murmured. Then he straightened his back and quickly reminded himself that these women were the enemy.

"Welcome," the three blue-finned mermaids said in unison.

"Nice harmony there," Jack commented. "I just hope you don't start up all those choruses again. I don't think I can take any more of that bit. Nice place you've got here," Jack said, admiring the dripping cave. "Where exactly are we?"

"We are beneath the island that is here but is not here," the three replied.

"Come again?" Jack asked.

"The place that resides in Davy Jones's locker but also rises to the air above the sea. You saw this island, and you wished to explore it. You are a courageous one," the blue-finned mermaids said together. "Not many have dared explore Isla Sirena, and fewer still have been invited to meet us in our lair. You intrigue us."

"You're a mite interesting yourself," Jack said, figuring these blue-finned mermaids were the leaders. The green-tailed creatures must be their army—if soft-looking fish-tailed girls could constitute an army. It was an odd thought, but he knew from the legends how dangerous these creatures could be. His own crew had succumbed to their powers. He wondered what the Red-tails were. Servants, maybe?

As he scanned the cavern he noticed a movement just out of the corner of his eye. It was a kind of flickering. He turned back to face the blue-tailed sirens and started. He could have sworn they had just shape-shifted. For a moment he was certain he had seen their arms as tentacles ending in sharp nasty claws and their shining scales covered in barnacles and boils. Yet when he looked at the mermaids dead-on they were beautiful again.

And now, he sensed the same thing happening with all the green-tailed mermaids just beyond his peripheral vision.

Steady on, he told himself. Keep your head clear.

"What is your name?" the three blue-tailed mermaids trilled.

"Jack Sparrow. Well, actually now, *Captain* Jack Sparrow. I've got a ship. The *Barnacle*. Little thing really, not such a . . ."

"Silence!" the three mermaids rang out in unison.

"So," he cleared his throat, "you know who I am. And now, I assume, you are the great Sirens of legend. Call sailors to their doom and all that," he said.

"No, Jack Sparrow. We are not the Sirens. We are the merfolk. We sing our own melody, and we do the bidding of the Sirens. We are their agents, like the sea beast you killed during the last rising sun. There are others you were fortunate enough not to encounter—gill men, sea warriors . . . We all receive the protection of the Sirens in return for our services."

"And what exactly *are* your services, pray tell?" Jack asked, leaning forward.

Three Blue-tails flicked their fins in unison. "Our song will tear open your heart, and you will beg for more. It will tease you with your greatest desire till you grow mad. And this desire will eventually burn so fierce that you will drive yourself directly to us. Then it is our charge to deliver you to those to whom we answer."

"The Sirens," Jack said.

"Yes," the Blue-tails replied.

Jack thought about this.

"So, that explains why Fitzy wants to go join the Light Brigade, Tumen wants to go home, Arabella threw herself overboard, and Jean wants that mangy feline transformed back into a human form—"

"—which is the feline's wish as well," the mermaids finished for Jack, "hence the eerily human posturing."

"But what about me? Why was I not affected?" He smiled smugly. "I guess it's likely because you fancy me," Jack said, smiling and tugging at his shirt collar. "Can't really say I blame you, ladies," Jack continued, examining his dirty fingernails proudly in an attempt to look nonchalant. Then he reminded himself that these ladies were not his friends.

"But you *were* affected, Jack Sparrow. Remember what you desire most. You were following what you desire most," they responded.

This was not clear to Jack, who shook his head in confusion.

"Your greatest desire . . ." all the mermaids in the cavern crooned.

"Desire," hundreds of them echoed over and over, "desire."

Jack bit his lip. He was going to have to think about this one for a while.

"Well, no harm done," he told the merfolk. "I'd have acted the same way with or without your musical interference." He took a step closer to the edge of the lagoon. "But now I really must insist. Release my crew and my ship from your spell . . . or else."

Jack noticed the leaders' blue tails flicking the way Constance's tail did when she was about to pounce. He braced himself for an attack and gripped his sword, which still stank of slain sea beast.

"We are willing to make a deal," the three Blue-tails sang.

"A deal . . . a deal . . . a deal . . ." the others chimed in.

"I can do without the chorus, please," Jack said. "No offense."

"None taken," the mermaids replied.

He turned to address the entire circle of Green-tails and once again was startled by strange transformations in his peripheral vision. Claws snapped; what had seemed to be pretty, soft faces grew scaly and fanged; tentacles reached toward him, then retracted. With a nervous shiver, he faced the Blue-tails again.

"You were saying," he said, his voice a little shaky.

"We will let you and your crew continue unimpeded on one condition. You must offer to us the greatest treasure you will ever obtain."

Jack flinched—he already considered the Sword of Cortés as good as his. The prospect of cutting this deal so he was free to search for the Sword just to lose it again to the Sirens was unthinkable.

"I'm afraid on that I shall have to disappoint you," he told them. "I see no profit in going through all the trouble of finding the Sword of Cortés, risking the life of my crew—not to mention my own—endure great hardship, and face who knows what obstacles just to turn it over to you lot." He shook his head. "We'll have to do a bit more negotiating, my dears. The Sword of Cortés is not a treasure I'm going to part with."

All the mermaids in the cavern laughed, their amused voices trilling. The sound was echoing so loudly in the huge cavern that Jack had to force himself not to cover his ears.

"Not all treasure is silver and gold,

Jack Sparrow," the Blue-tails said.

Jack wondered why these supernatural types always found the need to speak in riddles. He could hardly figure out what his greatest *desire* was, and now he was challenged to come up with the thing that would be the greatest *treasure* he'd ever obtain. And that, only to barter it away in order that he and his crew could sail on, in search of the treasure he desired most . . . which he'd have to return to the merfolk once it was procured. It was all so confusing.

"Well," Jack said, "if it's not silver and gold you're looking for, then it *can't* be *that* important. I accept your offer," Jack said. All the mermaids below Isla Sirena hissed.

"Then we have made a deal," the Blue-tails sang.

"Great, then. Be on my way now," Jack said. "Can any one of you be a lady and show me the way out?" he asked, winking at a particularly cute Red-tail, who smiled back.

"Before we release you, we require collateral," the Blue-tails countered.

"Sorry, Scaly Tails, got nothing on me but this old sword, my boots, and old Stone-Eyed Sam's stone eye."

The coven gasped.

"We will take the eye."

Jack shrugged. He'd taken it as a souvenir of his last adventure, but it didn't have any value beyond the sentimental. And Jack Sparrow was anything but sentimental. He held out the stone that was once set in the skull of the pirate Stone-Eyed Sam and dropped it neatly into one of the Blue-tails' hands. The mermaids smiled with pleasure.

"Very well. We will hold this stone until you return to deliver to us your most prized treasure."

Jack shrugged. "Okay, then," he said. These mermaids were not quite as clever as they thought they were.

The mermaids grinned at Jack as though they could read his thoughts. A sudden shiver shot up Jack's spine. Their identical smiles unnerved him. He shook off the strange feeling of doom.

"Jack Sparrow," the Blue-tails said, then paused . . .

Jack stared at them, waiting.

"You are *free* to go," they finished, laughing.

"Free, free, free," the rest of the coven repeated, as the word echoed throughout the cavern.

Jack felt a hot rush of blood go to his head. *Free.*

Freedom was what Jack treasured most. It is why he couldn't be enslaved by the mermaids' song. It was also what he had just bartered away.

The evil cackling resounded through the cavern as a Green-tail's head emerged from the water. Up close, Jack could clearly see the scales on her face. She reached out and led Jack to the funnel of the whirlpool that had brought Jack to their lair. The Green-tail blew Jack a mocking kiss, then guided him back into the whirlpool where he was instantly sucked back up to the surface. He popped his head out of the water and quickly found the *Barnacle*.

He turned to catch one more glimpse of Isla Sirena, but it was already vanishing. He felt the deep, sudden pain of regret. He knew the next time he saw the island, he would be imprisoned there, possibly forever. He swallowed hard and dragged himself back aboard the *Barnacle*.

# CHAPTER ELEVEN

*O*nce he was back on his boat, Jack saw that things were, as he had hoped, back to normal.

"Help!" Arabella screamed. "Jack, where are you?"

"Untie us!" Fitzwilliam yelled.

"Jack, help us! Somebody knocked us out and tied us up," Jean hollered.

Constance mewed and hissed, and Tumen struggled silently.

Jack stepped into the view of his crew and began to untie them.

"Jack!" Arabella cried. "You're alive!"

"What has happened here?" Fitzwilliam asked.

"Oh, just the usual mayhem," Jack said. "Nothing to fret about. It's all over now. Captain Jack has set everything right. And now we'll all need to set this ship back on course."

"Why are we tied to the mast? Who did this to us?" Fitzwilliam demanded to know.

"It was for your own safety," Jack said, explaining no further and quickly untying the tangled ropes that held his crew. "Now we must find our bearings. I believe we are far off course."

"Tumen and I will check the charts and our sightings," Jean said. Tumen nodded, and together they went to the helm and began studying the instruments.

Jack gazed down at Constance. The cat

stared up at him. "I'm tempted to keep this one tied up," he said.

"Oh, no, you won't!" Jean said. "She is as much a member of this crew as the rest of us."

"Oh, all right," Jack relented. He knelt down and loosened the rope around the cat. She quickly scrambled to the prow to keep watch over the sea.

"We're both wet," Arabella said to Jack, gazing down at her still-damp dress. "Why?"

"I had some business underwater," Jack said.

"What about me?" Arabella asked.

"You—you were looking for something you thought might be found in the sea. I persuaded you otherwise."

"Oh."

"We're having trouble finding our course," Jean called from the helm.

"Why am I not surprised," Jack mumbled.

"You!" Fitzwilliam pointed at Jack accusingly. "You have gotten us off course, you have tied us to a mast, and you almost had us killed, first by a notorious pirate and then by a raging sea beast."

"Don't forget the mermaids," Jack said.

"What mermaids do you speak of?" Fitzwilliam asked.

"Never mind that," Jack said. "Now, please make your point and make it quickly."

"My point is," Fitzwilliam began, "that this mission is a sham. You are not . . ."

". . . a captain . . . I know, I know . . ." Jack finished for him.

Fitzwilliam opened the chest on the deck where the crew kept their most precious treasures, including the scabbard that belonged to the Sword of Cortés. He waved

120

the scabbard in Jack's face and said, "For all we know there is absolutely nothing different about this scabbard than any other!" Fitzwilliam angrily threw the scabbard to the deck. The crew watched in wonder as the scabbard spun around—and *gained* momentum instead of losing it. It began to waver a bit and then steadied itself in one direction. Jack and Fitzwilliam looked at each other.

"Okay . . ." Jack said, pulling out his compass, which, like everything else on the ship, was again in working order. "Well, the scabbard is not pointing north . . ."

". . . but it is pointing in a consistent direction . . ." Arabella said. Each time she tried to move the scabbard it sprang back to the position it had set itself in.

". . . which can only mean . . ." Fitzwilliam said.

"... the scabbard is acting as a compass ..." Tumen added.

"... and there's only one thing I can think of it could be pointing toward ..." Jean said.

"The Sword of Cortés!" Jack shouted triumphantly. "Crew ... set a thataway sort of course! We are about to become very rich, very powerful ..." He paused and thought for a moment, then he smiled and finished, "... and very free."

## Captain's Log

I am now one of the few men ever to match wits with the Sirens' mermaids and live to tell the ~~tail~~ tale. This bit about returning to them to give up my freedom has me a little concerned. Though not entirely. After all, I am Captain Jack Sparrow, and Captain Jack Sparrow can find his way out of any mess. So, for now, we're back on course—thanks to my brilliant, clever, quick-thinking action to throw the sheath of the Sword of Cortés to the ground, which, I knew, would cause it to act as a compass. Now there is nothing to stand between us and finding Louis . . . and the Sword.

_Captain Jack Sparrow_

*Don't miss the next volume in the continuing adventures of Jack Sparrow and the crew of the mighty Barnacle.*

# Vol. 3: The Pirate Chase

Jack and company are hot on the trail of Left-Foot Louis. But chasing down a fierce seafarer is challenging, even for Jack's formidable crew. And to top it all off, Arabella has a personal score to settle with Louis, but doing so could jeopardize the entire mission!